# WE BOTH READ®

## Withdrawn

## Parent's Introduction

*We Both Read* is the first series of books designed to invite parents and children to share the reading of a story by taking turns reading aloud. This "shared reading" innovation, which was developed in conjunction with early reading specialists, invites parents to read the more sophisticated text on the left-hand pages, while children are encouraged to read the right-hand pages, which have been written at one of three early reading levels.

Reading aloud is one of the most important activities parents can share with their child to assist their reading development. However, *We Both Read* goes beyond reading *to* a child and allows parents to share reading *with* a child. *We Both Read* is so powerful and effective because it combines two key elements in learning: "showing" (the parent reads) and "doing" (the child reads). The result is not only faster reading development for the child, but a much more enjoyable and enriching experience for both!

Most of the words used in the child's text should be familiar to them. Others can easily be sounded out. You may find it helpful to read the entire book aloud yourself the first time, then invite your child to participate on the second reading. Also note that the parent's text is preceded by a "talking parent" icon: ☺ ; and the child's text is preceded by a "talking child" icon: ☺ .

*We Both Read* books is a fun, easy way to encourage and help your child to read—and a wonderful way to start your child off on a lifetime of reading enjoyment!

We Both Read: Too Many Cats

--------------------------------------------------

Text Copyright © 2003 by Sindy McKay
Illustrations Copyright ©2003 Meredith Johnson
*All rights reserved*

Published by
Treasure Bay, Inc.
P.O. Box 119
Novato, CA 94948 USA

PRINTED IN SINGAPORE

Library of Congress Catalog Card Number: 2003105919

Hardcover ISBN-10: 1-891327-49-6
Hardcover ISBN-13: 978-1-891327-49-0
Paperback ISBN-10: 1-891327-50-X
Paperback ISBN-13: 978-1-891327-50-6

**We Both Read® Books**
Patent No. 5,957,693

Visit us online at:
**www.webothread.com**

PR 11-09

WE BOTH READ®

# Too Many Cats

By Sindy McKay

Illustrated by Meredith Johnson

TREASURE BAY

It was the day before Suzu's birthday and Suzu knew just what she wanted. It was not a bike, or skates, or even the red hat her mother made her try on at the store.

Suzu wanted . . .

. . . a white cat.

Suzu told her mother that she wanted a cat and her mom said, "We'll see."

So Suzu was pretty sure she was going to get a new . . .

. . . red hat.

Still, Suzu was hopeful. She went to bed early that night to dream about the white cat she probably wasn't going to get. But before she fell asleep, she saw something moving in her bed. She pulled back the covers and found . . .

. . . one white cat!

It was just what Suzu wanted! But Suzu barely had time to say "HOORAY!!" when another cat crawled out from under her bed.

First Suzu had no cats. Then she had one cat. And now there were . . .

. . . two cats!

Suzu was surprised to hear a loud "meow" coming from the living room. Could it be ANOTHER cat??

She crept into the living room and looked around. There, on top of the TV, curled up in a little furry ball, was . . .

. . . a red cat.

Suzu could hardly believe her eyes!

First there was a white cat ON her bed, then a black cat UNDER her bed, and now a red cat on top of the TV. That made one, two . . .

. . . three cats!

Suzu felt a little silly for doubting that her mother was going to get her a cat. It seemed her mother was planning to give her THREE cats for her birthday!

But wait. What was that sound in the kitchen? Could it be that her mother was going to give her . . .

. . . four cats?

Suzu hurried to the kitchen, but was a little disappointed when she didn't see another cat. Then she heard a tiny "meow" coming from the cupboard. She opened the cupboard door and there was . . .

. . . a yellow cat.

Suzu went to hug the yellow cat, but stopped when she heard a crashing sound behind her. She turned to see that the curtain had been pulled down from the window.

Tangled up inside the curtain she spied . . .

. . . a green cat.

Suzu's mother had certainly found some unusual cats to give to Suzu! There was a white one, a black one, a red one, a yellow one, and a green one.

That made one, two, three, four . . .

. . . five cats!

Suzu gathered up all five of the amazing cats and started to carry them back to her bedroom. While passing through the dining room, a flash of color caught her eye. Stretched out lazily inside the china cabinet she spied . . .

. . . a purple cat!

Now Suzu's mind was reeling! Where were all these cats coming from? She had only asked for one.

But now she had one, two, three, four, five . . .

. . . six cats.

Suzu picked up cat number six and moved cautiously through the living room, hoping this cat was the last.

Then Suzu felt something pawing her hair. She looked up to find another cat. And this one was PINK!

That made it one, two, three, four, five, six . . .

. . . seven cats.

Suzu couldn't believe it. Now there was one cat on the chandelier, two cats climbing in the potted plants, three cats crammed inside of Mom's favorite vase, and one more on Dad's special rocking chair.

All that was bad enough, but then Suzu spied . . .

. . . a blue cat.

Have you ever seen a cat that's blue? Neither had Suzu! She hurried toward her bedroom, hoping with all her might that this was the last cat she would see tonight.

Trotting behind Suzu were one, two, three, four, five, six, seven . . .

. . . eight cats!

Suzu was almost to her bedroom when she heard another crash. She tried to ignore it, but she couldn't. So she rushed into the bathroom and pulled back the shower curtain. You can guess what Suzu saw.

Now there were one, two, three, four, five, six, seven, eight . . .

. . . nine cats.

Suzu sprinted to her room. She did NOT want to find any more cats! She jumped onto her bed and another cat bounced into the air. This one had stripes with all the colors of the rainbow.

One, two, three, four, five, six, seven, eight, nine . . .

. . . ten cats.

Enough already! Suzu loved cats. But ten cats were more than she could handle. What was her mother thinking?

Suzu climbed under her covers, pulled them up high over her head, and thought again about what she had found.

One, two, three,
four, five, six, seven,
eight, nine, ten cats!

Suzu felt someone shaking her shoulder
and softly calling, "Suzu? It's time to get up.
Today is your birthday!"

Suzu carefully peeked out from her covers
and looked around for the cats. But instead
of ten cats, Suzu saw . . .

. . . no cats.

Suzu was very confused. First she wanted one cat. Then she found ten cats. Now there were no cats at all.

Suzu's mother whispered, "I have a surprise for you."

She pulled something white and fluffy from behind her back and Suzu smiled. It was just what she wanted!

One white cat!

If you liked *Too Many Cats*, here is another
We Both Read® Book you are sure to enjoy!

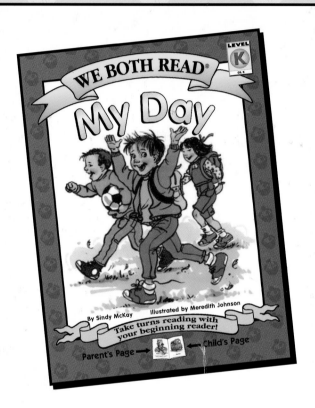

This Level K book is designed for the child who is
just being introduced to reading. The child's pages
have only one or two words, which relate directly to
the illustration and even rhyme with what has just
been read to them. This title is a charming story
about what a child does in the course of a simple
happy day.